Stories Children Love

The Woods beyond the Wall

by
W.G. Van de Hulst

illustrated by
Willem G. Van de Hulst, Jr.

INHERITANCE PUBLICATIONS
NEERLANDIA, ALBERTA, CANADA
PELLA, IOWA, U.S.A.

Library and Archives Canada Cataloguing in Publication
Hulst, W. G. van de (Willem Gerrit), 1879-1963
[Bengels in het bos. English]
 The woods beyond the wall / by W.G. Van de Hulst ; illustrated
by Willem G. Van de Hulst, Jr. ; [translated by Harry der Nederlanden].
(Stories children love ; 8)
Translation of: Bengels in het bos.
Originally published: St. Catharines, Ontario : Paideia Press, 1978.
ISBN 978-1-928136-08-8 (pbk.)
 I. Hulst, Willem G. van de (Willem Gerrit), 1917-, illustrator
II. Nederlanden, Harry der, translator III. Title. IV. Title:. Bengels in het
bos. English V. Series: Hulst, W. G. van de (Willem Gerrit), 1879-1963
Stories children love ; 8
PZ7.H873985Woo 2014   j839.313'62   C2014-903601-9

Library of Congress Cataloging-in-Publication Data
Hulst, W. G. van de (Willem Gerrit), 1879-1963.
 [Bengels in het bos. English.]
 The woods beyond the wall / by W.G. Van de Hulst ; illustrated by Willem G. Van de Hulst, Jr. ;
edited by Paulina Janssen.
  pages cm. -- (Stories children love ; #8)
 "Originally published in Dutch as De bengels in het bos. Original translations done by Harry der
Nederlanden and Theodore Plantinga for Paideia Press, St. Catharines-Ontario-Canada."
 Summary: While visiting their grandparents, Carla and Ria are to stay nearby because Grandma is
so worried about the busy highway beyond the woods, but two rowdy boys, Bert and Eddie, may
prove to be a bigger threat.
 ISBN 978-1-928136-08-8
 [1. Sisters--Fiction. 2. Grandparents--Fiction. 3. Behavior--Fiction. 4. Forests and forestry--
Fiction.] I. Hulst, Willem G. van de (Willem Gerrit), 1917- illustrator. II. Title.
PZ7.H887Woo 2017   [E]--dc23   2014017987

Originally published in Dutch as *De bengels in het bos*
Cover painting and illustrations by Willem G. Van de Hulst, Jr.
Original translation done by Harry der Nederlanden for Paideia Press,
St. Catharines-Ontario-Canada.
The publisher expresses his appreciation to John Hultink of Paideia Press
for his generous permission to use his translation (ISBN 0-88815-508-5).

Edited by Paulina Janssen

ISBN 978-1-928136-08-8

Contents

1. In Bed

"Shhh! Quiet!"

Ria poked Carla in her back.

They both slid down deeper under the covers.

Carla was giggling loudly.

"Shhh! Grandmother will hear you. See, I told you!"

Grandmother grumbled, "Go to sleep, girls! "

Oh, they lay so cozy in bed together. The built-in bed was just like a big coach. The curtains in front of the bed were open just a crack.

The light of the setting sun shone through the crack. It made a golden stripe on the back wall of the bed.

The two girls lay deep under the covers and they had such fun.

Carla said, "I know! Let's pretend we're two little birds in a nest. All right? Grandfather and Grandmother are the big birds. And they are flying off to fetch worms for us. Ha-ha-ha!"

"Shhh! Quiet! Grandmother will hear you."

And for a moment it was all quiet in the nest.

Carla and Ria, two little sisters, were staying with Grandfather and Grandmother for a while. Their father and mother were away on a trip.

Grandfather was a game warden. His house was in the middle of the woods.

Behind the house was a big garden, with peas, carrots, beans, cabbages, and raspberry bushes.

In front was a small flower garden with a green hedge and a white gate.

A sidewalk of yellow bricks led from the gate to the front door.

Outside the gate, a winding path began that led through the woods and to the dangerous world beyond.

Grandmother was very afraid of that dangerous world.

She said, "Be careful, children. Never go to the end of the path. Never! It leads out on the busy highway. And that highway is filled with speeding cars and motorbikes. Oh, it makes me afraid just thinking of it. If you go there, you'll get hurt for sure! And I promised your father and mother that I would look after you. So never go to the end of the path. Never!"

Grandmother, sitting at the table, sighed, "Ah, those poor little lambs!"

Grandfather grumbled in his deep voice, "Poor nothing. They're a couple of brave children."

Grandmother was worried.

The two girls were cuddled together warm and safe in the big bed.

Ria whispered, "Let's pretend the bed is a big car, all right?"

And Carla whispered back, "Yes, and we're riding down the winding path and out onto the highway with all the other cars and motorbikes. I'll drive."

She poked her elbow into Ria's ribs.

"Ouch!" said Ria. "Be careful!"

Grandmother heard the whispering. "What's this? Are you two still whispering? Go to sleep."

Hugging each other with delight, they rode along in their big car, out into the dangerous world.

That night the moon shone through a crack between the curtains into the big bed. The two little sisters  were asleep. Carla was clutching the covers with both hands. She must be dreaming that she was still driving the big car.

2. On the Wall

Then — one beautiful morning . . .
The little girls were playing in the garden behind the house.
"Good," thought Grandmother. "It's safe back there. The garden is far from the dangerous world beyond the woods. Good."

Behind the garden stood a crumbling old wall with a wooden door in it. But that door was locked. Yes, Grandmother's little lambs were safe.

Grandmother had found an old doll in the attic. She told them, "Long ago this doll belonged to your mother. You see, long ago your mother was a little girl too. So the doll is very old, but she's still very pretty. Her name is Caroline."

"I know!" Carla said. "Let's make Caroline even prettier."
"Even prettier? How?"
"We'll pick a big bunch of carrot tops. See? Grandmother won't mind. I've got a piece of string and I'll tie them around her waist. See? Then she'll have a pretty green skirt. Should we?"
The girls worked hard and played happily. They made the old doll even prettier.
"Isn't this fun?"

But then — on that beautiful morning . . .
Suddenly two little boys were sitting on top of the old wall. They were sitting right over the little door. They had climbed onto the wall from the trees. They often climbed the old wall.

But then . . . They saw two little girls in the garden. That was strange! They had never seen them before. The one boy — Eddie — wanted to go away. "Look! Girls! Let's go," he whispered.

But the other boy — Bert — said, "Why? Let's stay."

So they boldly remained sitting on the wall.

The girls looked up, startled.

Boys on the wall? Strange boys? What were they doing there?

Grandmother would not like that.

And Grandfather would not either.

If he saw them . . . !

Carla was the boldest.

"Get off the wall!" she shouted. "Get off!"

Bert laughed. "Why? It isn't your garden!" He crossed his arms and swung his legs over the garden as if he was going to stay all day.

Eddie was not quite so bold. He hung back a little. But he laughed too.

"Are you going to get off that wall?"

"No! Not for you! Listen. Can we come and play in the garden too?"

"No! Don't you dare!"

"Listen. We'll give you something. See? A nice, big, red one."

Bert rubbed a shiny red apple on his pants.

"No! And if you don't get off, I'll . . . !"

"Ha-ha-ha! Touch us if you dare! You don't even dare!"

Ria was getting angry. She shook her fist at the boys.

"I'll tell Grandfather. And he's the game warden!"

"Pooh! I'm not scared of your Grandfather."

But then . . .

Suddenly the two boys disappeared behind the wall, back into the woods.

The girls could not see them anymore but they heard them laugh and talk and sing.

Grandmother had come into the garden.

She scowled when she saw the boys. She shook her fist at those two bold little rascals on the wall.

That had scared them and they had quickly jumped off the wall back into the woods.

"Come, girls. Never mind those rowdy boys. I know them. They are Bert and Eddie, the miller's two boys. They are little rascals.

"Sometimes they go out on the highway — the dangerous highway with the speeding cars and motorbikes.

"Don't play with those boys. Don't go along with those boys. That's dangerous. Just like the highway.

"Come, girls. Grandmother will make you some pancakes. Would you like that?"

3. The Sun

It was nighttime. But — it wasn't dark yet.

The sun was going to bed but its golden beams still glittered between the black trees in the woods.

"Pretty, isn't it?" Grandmother said.

The girls looked.

They were tucked in the big bed. "Little girls must go to bed early," said Grandmother. But the curtains were still wide open. And Grandmother sat by the bed knitting and chatting.

"Pretty, isn't it?"

The golden beams of the sun shone between the trees into the little room and against the back wall of the bed.

Grandmother knitted. The girls were quiet. Carla, who was lying in the front of the bed, looked past her pillow to the blazing red archway in the distance and to the glistening hills of gold. She thought, "It is so beautiful, so beautiful. It looks like a city of gold."

"Grandmother, is that where the angels live? Is that Heaven?"

Grandmother stopped knitting.

Heaven? Ria, lying behind Carla, popped up to take a look.

"Heaven? Of course not, child. That's the sun going to bed beyond the woods. Heaven is much, much more beautiful than the sun. There the streets are made of gold."

It was quiet for a moment.

"Grandmother, are there cars and motorbikes in Heaven? And are they made of gold too?"

"Oh, silly girl! There is nothing dangerous in

14

Heaven. In Heaven there is nothing but happiness. Forever and ever."

Again it was quiet.
"Grandmother, have you ever been to Heaven?"
"Me? Of course not! What silly questions. But I do know about Heaven.
"Heaven is where God lives. Everything is beautiful and good and happy there. There is no sadness, no pain, and no danger. And no evil either. Heaven is much, much more beautiful than the sun."

Again it was quiet.
Ria laid down behind Carla again.
"Now it is time to go to sleep, girls. But first your prayers. Like this. Just like last night. All right?"

Grandmother sat beside the bed and put her hands on the blankets. The little girls put their hands in Grandmother's hands.

Grandmother prayed very softly. And the little girls listened with their eyes closed.

"Lord, Thou lovest us all. Also Carla and Ria. Give them hearts that love Thee, for that is the most beautiful thing. Forgive all their sins. And make a place ready for them in Thy beautiful Heaven."

4. Caroline

Morning had come.

Carla and Ria were playing — in the woods. They had gone through the little door in the old wall behind the garden. But they had asked Grandmother first.

"Well, all right," said Grandmother. "There are no cars and motorbikes in the woods. But be careful! Don't go too far or you will get lost."

Ria had an idea. As she walked, she traced a wiggly line on the path with a big stick.

"Smart, isn't it? Then we won't get lost."

Carla also had an idea. She put Caroline, the old

doll, against the trunk of a pine tree. The ground was covered with a thick blanket of pine needles and pinecones.

"Like this. Then she'll be warm and cozy."

Carla covered Caroline with pine needles. Only her head with her pale cheeks and her red cap were left sticking out. Ria helped.

Then they put the pinecones around the little pile of pine needles. They gathered little green twigs and stuck them in the pile too. Then it looked very beautiful.

"Isn't that nice Caroline? Isn't that warm and cozy?"

Suddenly Carla poked Ria.

"Shhh! Look, over there!" Carla whispered excitedly. Ria looked. On one of the paths in the

woods sat a little squirrel with a bushy tail. He looked at the girls and then scooted away into the bushes. Too bad!

"Come on!" whispered Carla.

She quickly tiptoed down the path to find the squirrel.

Ria was frightened. "What if he bites?"

But she followed Carla anyway, on her tippytoes. Very carefully. They looked and looked and called for him. They pushed through the bushes and caught a glimpse of him scooting up a tree. Then he was gone again.

"Nasty squirrel," Carla grumbled.

They went farther and farther, from one path to another. But they could not find the little squirrel anywhere.

"Come on. Let's go back to Caroline," Ria said.

Oh, but which way did they have to go? They went this way and that way. They paled with fear. They looked and looked.

Then . . . at last! There was the wiggly line that Ria had traced on the path. Oh, then they knew where they were.

They hurried around the bend.

Oh, and there — yes, there, under the tree, was Caroline. Oh, but . . . !

The girls stood still, shocked. There was Caroline, but the twigs and cones were all messed up. And there were pine needles in Caroline's hair. What had happened? Who could have done that?

The little girls looked around in fear. Could some animal have done that? A wolf maybe? Or a bear? No, that couldn't be, could it? After all, there were no wolves or bears in the woods. But who could have done it then?

"Come on, let's go home!" Carla said, grabbing the doll. "Let's go!"

Carla tried to pull Caroline out from under the tree. But Caroline did not move. The doll was stuck. Stuck?

How could that be? What was holding their doll? Those poor little girls.

They were getting more and more frightened. They kept looking around in fear. Their hands shook.

The doll's one leg was held by a piece of string. And the string was tied to a root of the tree.

The little girls pulled, but the string would not let go. They had to get Caroline loose! They had to! They couldn't leave her in the woods all alone!

Oh, the frightened little girls fell to their knees and together they fumbled at the string on the doll's leg. One of the doll's little red shoes fell off. But the girls did not see it.

Hurry, hurry! They had to get away! Far away! Suddenly the quiet woods had become very scary. Hurry, hurry! Run, run!

"The woods . . . huff . . . are dangerous . . . huff . . . too!" Ria panted.

"Yes . . . huff . . . yes!" Carla panted.

Back to the old wall. Through the little door. They slammed it shut. Through the garden to the house.

Grandmother was sitting in the sun on the bench behind the house. She was darning Grandfather's socks.

"Grandmother! Grandmother! Listen!"

5. The Winding Path

"Let's go look at the highway. Just a quick look."
Ria looked shocked. "But we may not!"
"We won't go on it. We'll just go where we can see
it. Come on!"
They went. They walked very carefully, as if the
winding path was also dangerous. They kept looking
back to see if Grandmother was watching. But the
path was too windy.
"Come on!" Carla whispered.
Soon they came to the highway. They were tiptoeing
now. Oh, the road was very quiet. There was no one
in sight.
"It isn't dangerous at all," Carla said. "Let's walk
along it. Just a little way."

"Aren't you scared?"

"Me? No! There's no one in sight."

"Yes, but what if . . ."

Carla saw a matchbox lying in the grass. She picked it up. It rattled. "Oh, look! There are matches in it. We'll give it to Grandmother."

"Yes!" Ria said.

Carla tucked it away in the pocket of her dress.

Far down the road came a man on a bicycle. Ria drew back into the woods, onto the path. But Carla stayed by the road. Who was scared of a bicycle? But then . . .

Suddenly, out of the bushes on the other side of the road burst a little pig. He dashed across the road. Behind the little pig two boys also burst out of the

bushes. They were chasing the little pig and they, too, dashed across the road.

They were catching up. The smaller boy grabbed the pig's curly tail and the bigger boy grabbed him around the neck. "I got you, you little runaway!"

Roaring down the road came a big truck. The boys calmly stood by the side of the road as the truck roared by.

The girls looked on. Oh, their cheeks turned red. Those were the boys that had been on the wall! They walked right across the highway, carrying the little pig.

And . . . and they were coming straight toward the two girls.

The boys laughed. Bert, the bigger one, tried to put the little pig in Ria's arms. "Here, you hold him. He'll make a nice doll. A lot nicer than that ugly blockhead doll that you have."

But Ria shuddered. She threw up her arms and screamed.

Carla was frightened too. She pushed Bert back. "Go away, you nasty boy! Go away!"

But . . . the little pig slipped out of Bert's arms again and ran as fast as he could down the winding path, his curly little tail bobbing up and down.

He disappeared into the bushes beside the path.
"Catch him! Catch him!" the boys shouted.

They dashed after him — down the winding path and into the bushes.
The slippery little pig had escaped from his pen beside the windmill.

"Catch him! We have to bring him back!"

6. The Octopus Tree

The sudden uproar frightened Carla and Ria. They ran back down the winding path, back to Grandmother. The matchbox rattled in Carla's pocket. The two boys had disappeared. Good! They were such rowdy boys. But they were somewhat nice too.

The girls peered into the bushes. The two boys and the little pig had disappeared.

But as they came around a bend in the winding path, what did they see in the middle of the path?

24

"Oh! The little pig!"

He stared at them with his beady little eyes, as if to say, "Catch me. Catch me if you can."

Catch him? Catch that horrible little beast? Oh, never! Never!

They did not dare go past him.

They stopped and huddled close together. What if he came after them? What if he tried to bite them? Should they call the boys? The boys must still be nearby, looking in the bushes. Should they?

Oh . . . ! Then . . .

A bicycle bell rang behind them, around the bend. The bicycle was still out of sight.

But . . . at once a gruff voice sounded. A deep, angry voice. They knew that voice. It was Grandfather!

He had come from the highway down the winding path. And he had seen everything.

He had seen the boys come back out of the bushes. He had seen the little pig. He had seen the frightened girls. He stopped.

"What are you boys doing in these woods?" He was very angry at the boys. "You rowdy little rascals! What is going on? First you climb on my wall. Then you tie the girls' doll to a tree. Don't deny it! And now you chase a pig into the woods. Pick up your pig and go! Don't let me catch you in these woods again! Next time I'll stuff you into the octopus tree. Do you understand? Now, pick up your pig and go! Right now!"

The little pig tried to run.

But the two boys were quick. They grabbed their pig and hurried away down the winding path back to the highway. "Come on, girls," said Grandfather. "We are going home too."

"Grandfather, what is the octopus tree?"

"Do you not know about the terrible octopus tree? Everyone around here knows about the octopus tree. Those little rascals do too. And everyone is scared of the octopus tree."

"What kind of tree is it?"

"Someday you will have to go look for it in the woods. It's a tree with a short, thick trunk, like a huge barrel. But out of the trunk grow several other big, thick branches, like octopus arms. And if you land between those branches, in the middle of those arms . . ."

"What, Grandfather? What?"

"Well, if you land in the hollow between those branches — listen good now — then those branches close up and you will never get out again. Isn't that terrible? Better stay away from it."

"Oh, Grandfather, and if those boys come into the woods again, are you really going to stuff them into the tree?"

"Oh, yes! Both of them!"

"But . . . but then they will never be able to get out again!"

"Shh! I'll tell you a secret about that octopus tree. If I tap on one of those branches — on the one called Clem, the one with the big knot — and if I say, 'All right, Clem, let them go,' then the branches open up again."

The girls asked no more questions. They walked next to Grandfather with glum faces. They were thinking about the octopus tree.

They did not see the twinkle in Grandfather's eyes. Grandmother was waiting at the front gate. "Hurry! Dinner is ready."

7. Hide-and-Seek

That afternoon . . .

The girls were back in the woods again. They were playing hide-and-seek.

"Now it's my turn to hide!" Ria said.

Carla leaned against a big tree with her hands over her eyes as she counted to one hundred. She was not allowed to see where Ria would hide.

While she counted, Carla pressed herself against the tree. Then suddenly she heard the matchbox crackle in her pocket. She had forgotten to give it to Grandmother. Oh, well, she could do that later.

"Hello! Hello there! Can we play too?"

There they were again, those rowdy boys, running through the woods. And Grandfather had said they were not supposed to be in the woods.

The girls were shocked.

"You better go away. If Grandfather catches you, he'll stuff you into the octopus tree, and then . . ."

"Pooh!" scoffed Bert. "Your grandfather can't catch us anyway. We can run faster than him. And we can run even faster if we take off our shoes. Pooh! We're not scared of your grandfather at all. We want to play too. Eddie and I will go hide and you two girls will come and find us. Yes? Stand against a tree and hide your eyes. No peeking! Come on, Eddie."

The girls . . . ?

They were a little fearful, but the new game sounded like fun. Should they play with the boys? Just for a little while?

"Come on!" said Carla. She leaned against a tree. Ria, a little fearful and uneasy, leaned against the tree too. They hid their eyes and counted to one hundred.

Then they had to find the boys. They were nowhere to be seen.

"Come on!" said Carla. "We'll find them."

The girls looked and looked. They looked everywhere. But where were the boys?

They were nowhere to be seen. They were gone. Strange! The quiet woods suddenly seemed very scary.

"Do you see anything?" Ria whispered.

"No!" Carla whispered back. "Nothing. Isn't that strange?"

8. Strange!

Swish! Crackle! Crash!

What was that? There! Up there!

Two dark shapes suddenly scooted down the trunk of two tall pine trees.

They were Bert and Eddie! They tumbled to the ground. But then they scrambled up and dashed away like frightened mice. They ran as fast as they could — into the bushes and into the woods.

But why? What had happened?

Bert and Eddie had climbed up high in the pine trees to hide. The old branch stumps made the trees easy to climb. And the girls had looked only on the ground, so it was a good hiding place.

But . . . the girls did not know that the two rowdy boys sitting high up in the trees could see much farther then they could on the ground.

And . . . the girls also did not know that suddenly far away the two climbers had seen Grandfather's green hat coming between the bushes.

The girls had no idea that the two little rascals suddenly became very frightened of the octopus tree, and so — swish, crackle, — they tumbled down and dashed off like two frightened mice chased by a cat.

"Aren't those boys strange?" Ria said. "I wonder why they were so frightened?"

"I don't know," said Carla. "It's too bad. Now our new game is spoiled. I don't feel like playing with just the two of us."

"Me neither."

9. "Should I?"

"Should we?"

Carla already had an idea for another game. "Should we make a house?"

"But how?"

"Like this. We'll make a big square with pinecones.

See? That will be the living room and that will be the kitchen. And the hallway will be over here."

Carla gathered an armload of pinecones. She knelt and began to put the prickly cones in a long, neat row. That would be the living room wall.

"Quick, Ria. Get some more, lots more. There are lots and lots of them over there."

Ria brought more — another armload.

"Isn't this nice!"

The girls had long forgotten the rowdy boys who had run away.

Ria was busy gathering more pinecones.

Carla was busy putting them in long rows to make the walls of the house.

Carla knelt. Crrr, crrrack! it went in Carla's pocket as she leaned forward.

Oh, the match box!

And then . . . ? Oh, that foolish, naughty Carla! Suddenly she forgot all about her beautiful house with the pinecone walls.

She pulled the matchbox from her pocket. She took a peek — just a little peek — inside the box.

When Ria came with another armload of pinecones, Carla whispered, "Should I?"

Ria stared with big eyes. She stared at the matchbox in Carla's hand and at the match in Carla's other hand — at the thin white stick with the little red cap. Ria was a little frightened, but she was also fascinated.

"Should I? Just one?" Scrrrape! went the little red cap along the rough side of the box. Scrrrape! Suddenly an orange flame flared up at the end of the thin, white stick.

It frightened Carla. Startled, she dropped the burning match.

Then . . . oh, that foolish Carla! The little box in her other hand was half open. All the red caps of the matches were showing in the open end of the box. The little orange flame dropped into the open box right on the other red caps. And suddenly all the other matches burst into flame.

Fssst . . . thoop! A big flame.

Oooh! Horrible!
A big flame shot up out of the box, blazing fiercely. It frightened Carla horribly. She flung the burning box away from her, as far as she could.
Moaning, she pushed two of her fingers into her mouth. Oh, that sudden, sharp pain. Oooh! The big

flame had burnt Carla's fingers. Tears of pain sprang to her eyes.

"Ouch! Oh! Oh!"

Together they dashed away in fear and panic. They did not look back at the burning matchbox. Run, run! Away from that horrible flame.

Carla pushed her burnt fingers into her mouth as far as she could. But they still hurt.

She moaned to Ria, "Don't tell. Don't tell Grandmother!"

"No," Ria moaned back in fright. "No, I won't."

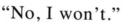

10. "Those Scoundrels Did It!"

The door in the old wall stood open. Oh, good! They ran through the garden and plopped down on the bench behind the house. Carla rocked with pain.

"Don't tell," she moaned.

"No, I won't."

Grandmother was in the kitchen.

But suddenly . . . Suddenly Grandfather burst into the garden through the little door in the wall.

He looked all flustered and he had lost his hat. He moved as fast as his old legs could carry him. He huffed and puffed.

He did not even see the girls. In frantic haste he rushed to the shed, grabbed his shovel, and turned back to the woods.

Grandmother saw him from the kitchen. "What is it? What is it?" she cried in fear. She was already standing in the doorway.

"The woods . . . huff . . . the woods . . . they're . . . huff . . . on fire! I . . . I tried to . . . huff . . . stamp it out. But . . . huff . . . I need a shovel. Those . . . huff . . . those little scoundrels from the windmill . . . they did it. I saw them . . . huff . . . up in the trees. If that fire gets away . . . !"

Huffing, he ran on.

"Be careful, you hear! Careful!" Grandmother

shouted after him. Frightened, she also rushed to the shed and also grabbed a shovel. She followed Grandfather as fast as her old legs could carry her. She was so frightened, she did not even see the girls. All she could think of was the fire, the fire in the woods. If it got into the trees, into the pine needles and pinecones . . . ! Everything was so dry in the summer. Then the beautiful little house would also go up in flames.

The little girls heard every word Grandfather said. Also what he said about the boys from the windmill. The poor little girls! They huddled together like two frightened little birds. They clung to the bench. Their throats ached with fear.
"Don't tell! Oh, don't tell!"

11. Frightened

That night . . .
The girls lay in the big bed. Far away between the trees the city of gold sent out its golden rays.

Grandfather and Grandmother sat at the table, just like the first night that the girls had slept in the big bed. Then it had been so nice behind the curtains — so safe, so cozy, so right.

But now? Now it was all spoiled.

Then they had been happy.

Now they were frightened.

Now it was no longer safe and cozy and right in the big bed.

The girls lay side by side in the dark. Their eyes were wide open. And also their ears.

They had said nothing about the matchbox. They were too frightened.

Grandfather and Grandmother were able to stop the fire.

They had come back very tired.

They were black with smoke and dust.

And they were very angry with the two boys.

Grandfather was still grumbling.

"I'll send the police after those wild rascals tomorrow. I have the crushed, half-burnt matchbox in my pocket. I found it under a tree."

The girls in the bed huddled closer together, more frightened than ever.

"Terrible! The whole forest might have gone up in flames. And the house too. Thank God the girls were home when the fire started. What if those poor dears had been caught in the fire!"

The girls slid still deeper under the covers. They trembled.

38

"The woods might have turned out to be even more dangerous than the highway. But I will get after those wild boys from the windmill tomorrow. That's for sure. I'm just too tired now. Tomorrow."

Deep under the covers the girls whispered to each other.
Carla said, "Shall we, Ria? Shall we?"
Ria said, "Aren't you frightened? I am."

Grandfather was still grumbling. "Those little scoundrels! Those reckless little scamps! Starting a fire in the woods! It's high time they were punished! Tomorrow."

Then a frightened, squeaky little voice came from the big bed, "Grandfather, please! We . . . we . . . !"
"Aren't you girls asleep yet?" Grandmother asked. "How can that be?"
Grandfather grumbled, "Oh, those poor girls are still upset by the fire."
"Grandfather, we . . . we . . . It was us. We started the fire."
"What?"
"You?"
Grandmother looked very shocked.
"You?" Her voice sounded very sad. "You? Such

sweet, such good little girls? But that can't be!"
Grandfather stood up. He came and sat down by the
bed. Very sternly, he said, "Come out from under
the covers and tell us what happened."

Then they told everything — everything.
About playing hide-and-seek with the boys who had
climbed up in the trees. About the house they had
made with pinecones. About the matchbox in Carla's
pocket. About the thin white match with the red cap.
About the orange flame that jumped into the box.
Their voices trembled with fright. Tears burned
40

behind their eyelids. Oh, how angry Grandfather would be!

But Grandfather? He said nothing. He went back to his place at the table. And he puffed on his pipe.

Grandmother tucked the girls back in.

"Oh, you foolish little girls! That was not very smart. That was very, very dangerous. You could both have been burnt. How terrible!

"You two did it and we blamed those boys. You should have told us right away.

"I'm glad you did tell us. That was good. Yes, that was very good. Now you must fold your hands and also tell the Lord what you did and ask Him to forgive you. Only then will everything be completely right. For the Lord who knows and sees everything will make it all right."

Carla gave Grandmother a quick kiss on the hand as she tucked the covers under her chin. Everything was right again. All her fear was gone.

Far away between the trees the blazing red archway of the sun shone and the hills glittered with gold. But Heaven, where the Lord heard the quiet prayers of the two foolish little girls, is much, much more beautiful than the sun.

12. A Party!

The next morning . . .
The girls were on their way to the windmill.
Grandmother walked with them through the woods.
At the little bridge she turned back. "See, there is
the windmill. Just follow that little road."

Bert and Eddie were playing in the yard in front of
the windmill.
At once someone shouted, "Grandfather wants to
see you boys!"
They looked up. Ah, there at the big gate were the
little girls from the woods. They were shouting
between the boards of the gate. The warden wanted
to see them? That frightened them.
"Why?"
"Because! Grandfather didn't say."
"No, we're not going. He'll stuff us into the octopus
tree."

"You have to come! Please?"

The girls wanted to tell the boys about Clem, the branch with the big knot. But they couldn't. It was a secret.

"Come on. You don't have to be scared."

The miller had overheard everything.

He said to his boys, "Go on, you little rowdies. Go with the girls. You did not set a fire in the woods yesterday, did you? I saw smoke yesterday."

"No, Father. We didn't."

The two little girls blushed.

"Well then, go on! The warden won't eat you. And if you've made trouble, into the octopus tree with you!"

Grandfather was sitting on the bench behind the house smoking his pipe.

Grandmother was busy at a little outdoor stove. Smoke was rising from the pipe on the back of the stove. What was Grandmother doing?

There came the children — all four of them.

The boys looked a bit frightened when they saw the game warden.

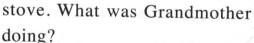

What would he do to them?

"Come over here," he said. They all sat beside him on the bench — the girls on one side and the boys on the other. The boys trembled a little.

Then Grandfather told them what happened yesterday. About the fire in the woods and about how terribly dangerous such a fire is.

"I said, 'Those two little rascals from the windmill must have started that fire. I saw them up in the trees.' But I was wrong. These two naughty girls did it. But they were honest and told us everything. Now everything is forgiven and forgotten. And I'm not angry with Bert and Eddie anymore either. I think you four little rascals ought to be friends."

Grandmother was busy at her little stove. She poured white batter into a big flat pan. The batter hissed and turned brown. And it smelled so delicious!

And then the party began! A party with big, thick pancakes filled with raisins and tiny bits of apple. Delicious! And the special syrup that Grandmother had made was also delicious.

First Grandfather got his pancake, then the boys, and then the girls. Sitting there waiting and smelling the pancakes — even that was delicious.

It was a wonderful party. The worry, the fear, the anger — they were all gone.

44

Carla looked at her fingers. They were still red, but the pain was gone too.

13. A Letter

Oh . . . the games they invented — those four rowdy little rascals playing in the woods. They kept making up wonderful new games.

Carla tore her dress once. And Ria lost her red ribbon. Caroline's nose was dented because she fell out of a tall tree. Bert scraped his knee and Eddie broke one of his wooden shoes. All four of them had scratches all over their legs from playing hide-and-seek among the raspberry bushes. But they looked forward to each day so they could play in the woods together.

But then — oh, then one day the mailman brought a letter. Carla and Ria's father and mother were back from their trip. They were going to come with the car and pick up their little girls.

"That's sad," Grandfather and Grandmother said.

"That's sad," Bert and Eddie said.

And the two girls? They were eager to see Father and Mother again. But they would also like to stay in the woods. If only Father and Mother lived in the woods too! Wouldn't that be wonderful!

On a beautiful morning it was time for them to leave. Grandfather and Grandmother walked them down the winding path to the highway. There the car was waiting for them.
The boys were there too. Of course! They had all become good friends.
"Good-bye! Good-bye!"

As the car drove away, the girls looked through the back window.
Bert thumbed his nose at them.
And Carla thumbed her nose at the boys.
That was funny. But it was also a little bit sad.
The boys slowly walked back down the winding path.
"How sad, isn't it?"
"Yes! It's sad!"
"But the warden said they were coming back again."
"That will be fun! I did like those girls."
"Yes, I did too!"

And then . . .
Then the woods were quiet again. Sometimes the boys would wander from the windmill across the

little bridge and into the woods. Grandfather did not chase them away anymore.

It was so quiet, so empty, so lonely in the woods and around the house.

The curtains in front of the built-in bed were always shut now, day and night.

Caroline was back in an old trunk in the attic. Her nose was dented and one of her little red shoes was gone.

But in the woods, under a layer of pine needles, lay something red. It was Caroline's other shoe. A pretty little snail had crawled inside it. Would it ever be found?

If the boys found it, you can be sure they would save it very carefully. For the girls were coming back. Grandfather had said so.

Titles in this series:

1. The Little Wooden Shoe
2. Through the Thunderstorm
3. Bruno the Bear
4. The Basket
5. Lost in the Snow
6. Annie and the Goat
7. The Black Kitten
8. The Woods beyond the Wall
9. My Master and I
10. The Pig under the Pew
11. Three Little Hunters
12. The Search for Christmas
13. Footprints in the Snow
14. Little Tramp
15. Three Foolish Sisters
16. The Secret Hiding Place
17. The Secret in the Box
18. The Rockity Rowboat
19. Herbie, the Runaway Duck
20. Kittens, Kittens Everywhere
21. The Forbidden Path